BULLDOZER'S
Christmas Dig

BULLDOZER'S

Candace Fleming
and Eric Rohmann

atheneum

A Caitlyn Dlouhy Book

ATHENEUM BOOKS FOR YOUNG READERS

New York   London   Toronto   Sydney   New Delhi

Christmas Dig

It was Christmas Eve,
and Dump Truck was carrying …
        carrying …
                carrying.

Digger Truck was stringing . . .
stringing . . .
stringing.

Crane Truck was lifting . . .
lifting . . .
lifting.

And Bulldozer was worrying . . .
worrying . . .
    worrying.

He didn't have any presents for his friends.
Not one. What could he do?

Looking out across the construction site,
he saw a tire half-buried in the snow.
"Hmmm," Bulldozer said to himself.
"I wonder what other treasures are under there?"
His blade rose.

He scooted across the snow.

"Now *this* looks like a place to dig!" Bulldozer exclaimed.

Scra-a-a-a-ape . . .

Scra-a-a-a-ape . . .

Scra-a-a-a-ape . . .

Thunk-bump!

"Treasure!" whooped Bulldozer.

But when he shoveled it out, all he saw was—
"Junk," grumbled Bulldozer.

Tossing it aside, he kept on digging.
Scra-a-a-a-ape . . .
Scra-a-a-a-ape . . .
Scra-a-a-a-ape . . .
Thunk-thud!

"Treasure?" hoped Bulldozer.

"More junk," he muttered.

Tossing it aside, he kept on digging.
Scra-a-a-a-ape . . .
Scra-a-a-a-ape . . .
Scra-a-a-a-ape . . .

Thunk-crunch!

"Please be treasure," begged Bulldozer.
But yet again, when he shoveled it out,
all he saw was—

"Arrgh!"
Bulldozer sighed.
Maybe there was no treasure.
But if there wasn't any treasure,
what would he give his friends?

He kept digging.
   Scra-a-a-a-ape . . .
         Scra-a-a-a-ape . . .
               Scra-a-a-a-ape . . .
The pile kept growing.
   Scra-a-a-a-ape . . .
         Scra-a-a-a-ape . . .
               Scra-a-a-a-ape . . .
It began to grow dark.
   Scra-a-a-a-ape . . .
         Scra-a-a-a-ape . . .
               Scra-a-a-a-ape . . .

   Bulldozer's hopes faded.

He dragged himself out of his hole.
He stared at the pile of junk, and his blade drooped.
"No Christmas treasure," sniffled Bulldozer.
"No presents for my friends."

Then, through the swirling, whirling,
twinkling snowflakes, he thought he saw—
Was it?
Could it be?

He pushed it that way.

He sat, smoke puffing from his stack for a moment.

Then he poked the pile this way.

He gave it a teensy nudge.

At last, he paused and looked at his work.

"Hmmm," said Bulldozer. "It needs one more thing."

He scooted across the snow.

His motor hummed a holiday song.

It was snowing hard when the big trucks
bumped over to where Bulldozer worked.

"It's quitting time!" boomed Dump Truck.

"Just one more minute,"
said Bulldozer.

"It's getting dark," rattled Scraper.

"And I'm getting cold," clattered Grader.

Bulldozer kept working.
"And it's Christmas Eve," clanged Crane. "It's..."

Bulldozer moved aside.

"For us?" rattled Cement Mixer.

"It's for all of you!" said Bulldozer.

"Now *that's* a present to treasure, kid," rumbled Roller Truck.

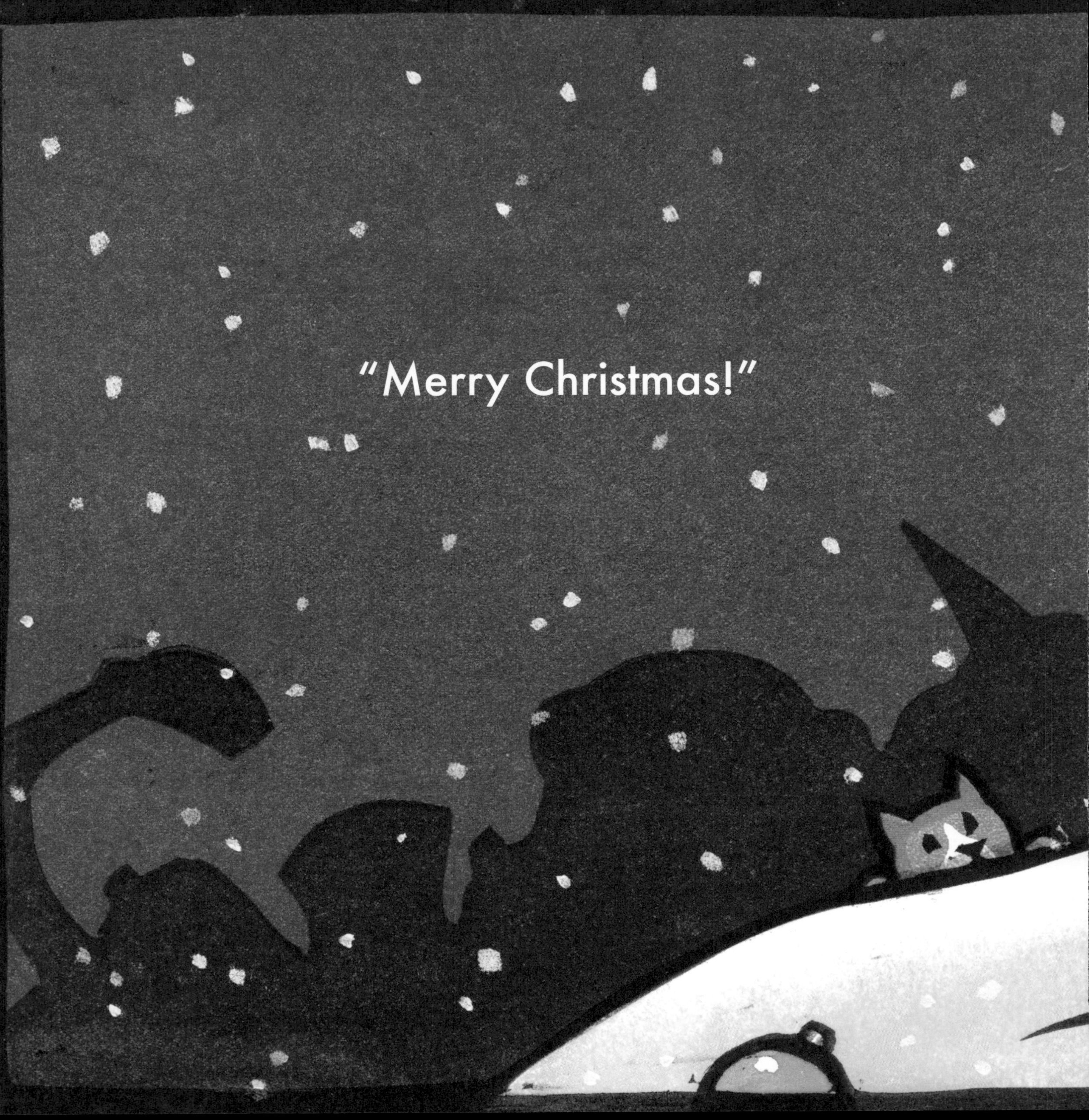

"Merry Christmas!"

To Caitlyn, our fearless foreman!
—E & C

ATHENEUM BOOKS FOR YOUNG READERS
An imprint of Simon & Schuster Children's Publishing Division
1230 Avenue of the Americas, New York, New York 10020
Text © 2021 by Candace Fleming
Illustrations © 2021 by Eric Rohmann
Book design by Karyn Lee © 2021 by Simon & Schuster, Inc.
ATHENEUM BOOKS FOR YOUNG READERS is a registered trademark
of Simon & Schuster, Inc. Atheneum logo is a trademark of Simon &
Schuster, Inc.
For information about special discounts for bulk purchases, please
contact Simon & Schuster Special Sales at 1-866-506-1949 or
business@simonandschuster.com.
The Simon & Schuster Speakers Bureau can bring authors to your live
event. For more information or to book an event, contact the Simon
& Schuster Speakers Bureau at 1-866-248-3049 or visit our website
at www.simonspeakers.com.
The text for this book was set in Futura BT.
The illustrations for this book were made using relief (block) prints.
Three plates were used for each image. The first two plates were
printed in multiple colors, using a relief printmaking process called
"reduction printing." The last plate was the "key" image, which was
printed in black over the color.
Manufactured in China
0621 SCP
First Edition
10 9 8 7 6 5 4 3 2 1
Library of Congress Cataloging-in-Publication Data
Names: Fleming, Candace, author. | Rohmann, Eric, illustrator.
Title: Bulldozer's Christmas dig / Candace Fleming ; illustrated by
Eric Rohmann. • Description: First edition. | New York : Atheneum
Books for Young Readers, [2021] | Series: The Bulldozer books
| "A Caitlyn Dlouhy Book." | Audience: Ages 4-8. | Audience:
Grades K-1. | Summary: "It's Christmas Eve and Bulldozer doesn't
know what to get his friends for Christmas. With a little creativity, he
will turn trash into treasure"—Provided by publisher. • Identifiers:
LCCN 2020057220 | ISBN 9781534438200 (hardcover) | ISBN
9781534438217 (eBook) • Subjects: CYAC: Bulldozers—Fiction.
| Construction equipment—Fiction. | Gifts—Fiction. | Christmas—
Fiction. • Classification: LCC PZ7.F59936 Bup 2021 | DDC [E]—dc23
• LC record available at https://lccn.loc.gov/2020057220